SOMETIMES A WALL...

BY DIANNE WHITE

illustrated by BARROUX

Owlkids Books

Owlkids Books acknowledges the financial support of the Canada Council for the Arts, the Ontario Arts Council, the Government of Canada through the Canada Book Fund (CBF) and the Government of Ontario through the Ontario Creates Book Initiative for our publishing activities.

Published in Canada by Owlkids Books Inc., 1 Eglinton Avenue East, Toronto, ON M4P 3A1
Published in the US by Owlkids Books Inc., 1700 Fourth Street, Berkeley, CA 94710

Library of Congress Control Number: 2019956933

Library and Archives Canada Cataloguing in Publication

Title: Sometimes a wall... | written by Dianne White ; illustrated by Barroux.
Names: White, Dianne, author. | Barroux, illustrator.
Identifiers: Canadiana 20200154788 | ISBN 9781771473736 (hardcover)
Classification: LCC PZ7.1.W55 Som 2020 | DDC j813/.6—dc23

Edited by Debbie Rogosin | Designed by Alisa Baldwin

Manufactured in Guangdong Province, Dongguan City, China, in April 2020, by Toppan Leefung Packaging & Printing (Dongguan) Co., Ltd.   Job #BAYDC77

A   B   C   D   E   F

Publisher of Chirp, Chickadee and OWL
www.owlkidsbooks.com

Owlkids Books is a division of bayard canada

For Stephanie Greene, who asked for a book about walls. With thanks, always, for the good conversations and friendship — D.W.

For Sophie Laure B. — B.

SO MANY KINDS OF WALLS TO SEE

CHALK WALL

SPILL WALL

ROCK WALL

HILL WALL

SO MANY WAYS A WALL CAN BE

WE WALL   SHOUT WALL

SOMETIMES A WALL
CAN COME BETWEEN

GATHER

SOMETIMES A PERSON
CAN BE MEAN

MISCHIEF

TAUNTS

WHISPERED LIES

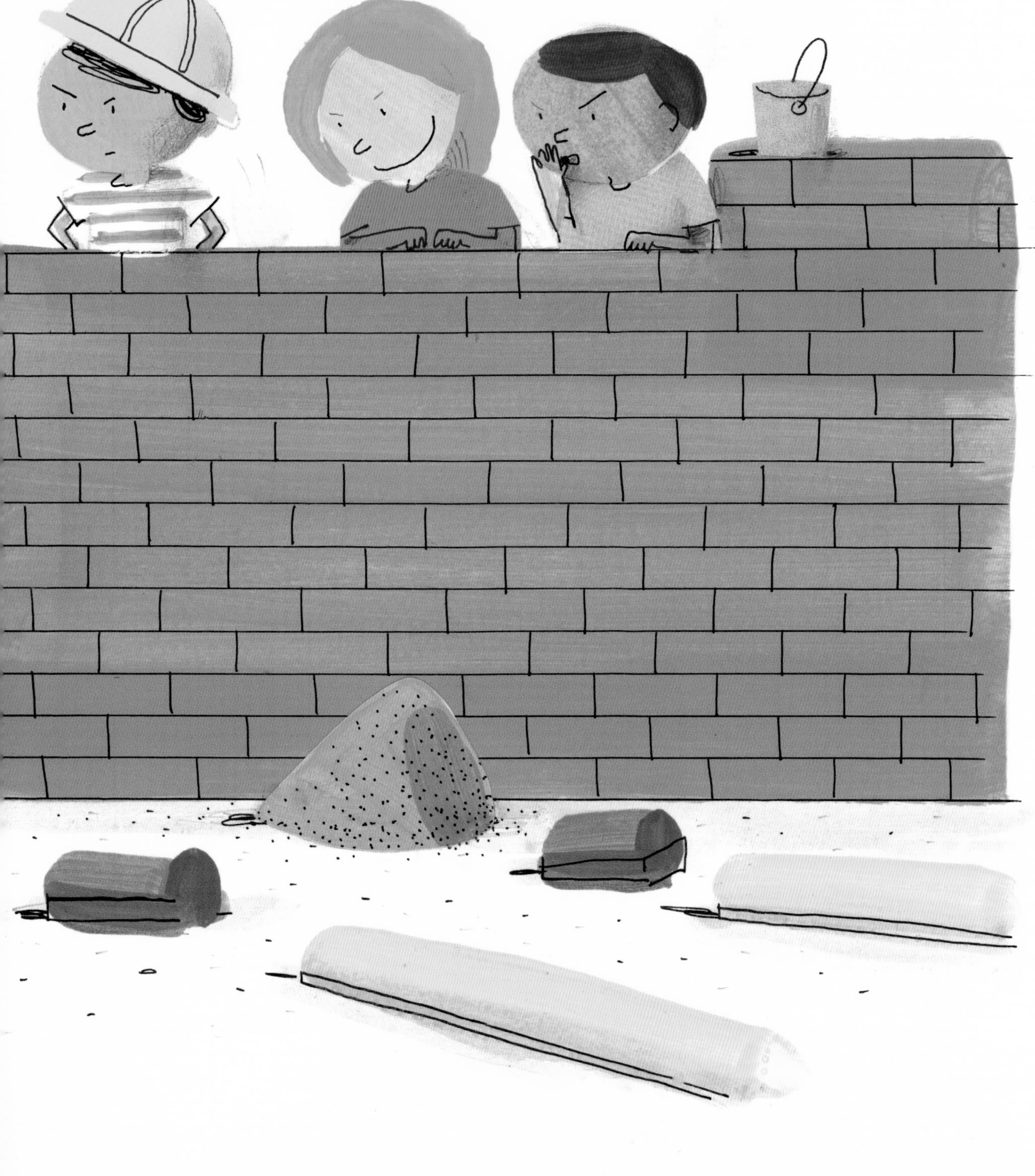

SO MANY THINGS
WE CHOOSE TO DO

STARE

SIGN

UNFAIR

DIFFERENT SIDES AND POINTS OF VIEW

— PLAY?

— STAY?

NO! —

GO! —

SO MANY FEELINGS
A WALL CAN BRING

ALONE

APART

REGRET

NEW START?

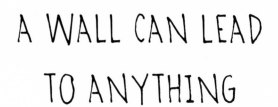

A WALL CAN LEAD TO ANYTHING

WAVE

WATCH

HOPEFUL

BRAVE

MEND

FRIENDS